The Ideas and Beliefs of Ancient Greece

Sally Cowan

The Ideas and Beliefs of Ancient Greece

Text: Sally Cowan
Editor: Ben Haskin
Design: James Lowe
Series design: James Lowe
Photo researcher: Corrina Tauschke
Production controller: Adam Bextream
Reprint: Siew Han Ong

Acknowledgements
The author and publisher would like to acknowledge permission to reproduce material from the following sources:
Akg-images: pp. 1, 3, 7, 10, cover; Alamy/Peter Oshkai: p. 9; Corbis: p. 12 (main); Corbis/Bettmann: pp. 14, 17; Corbis/Christophe Karaba/epa: p. 22 (inset); Corbis/Gianni Dagli Orti: p. 13; Corbis/Jon Arnold/Jai: p. 19; Corbis/The Gallery Collection: pp. 16, 20 (right); Getty Images: pp. 18, 21, 22, 23 (top right); iStockphoto/Nancy Nehring: pp. 21 (inset), cover; Julian Bruère © Cengage Learning Australia: pp. 4, 6; Photolibrary/Ed Eckstein: p. 12 (inset); Photolibrary/Herbert SA House Lank: p. 15; Photolibrary/Mary Evans Picture Library: p. 20 (left); Photolibrary/Science Photo Library: p. 11 (right); Photolibrary/The Bridgeman Art Library: pp. 5 (left), 8; Photolibrary/Tristram Kenton/Lebrecht: p. 23 (bottom); Shutterstock/Losevsky Pavel: p. 23 (top left); The Trustees of The British Museum: pp. 5 (right), back cover.

Every effort has been made to trace and acknowledge copyright. However, if any infringement has occurred, the publishers tender their apologies and invite the copyright holders to contact them.

Fast Forward Independent Texts
Level 23

For product information and technology assistance,
in Australia call 1300 790 853;
in New Zealand call 0508 635 766

For permission to use material from this text or product, please email **aust.permissions@cengage.com**

ISBN 978 0 17 018101 3
ISBN 978 0 17 017899 0 (set)

Cengage Learning Australia
Level 7, 80 Dorcas Street
South Melbourne, Victoria Australia 3205

Cengage Learning New Zealand
Unit 4B Rosedale Office Park
331 Rosedale Road, Albany, North Shore NZ 0632

For learning solutions, visit **cengage.com.au**

Printed in Australia by Ligare Pty Ltd
4 5 6 7 23 22 20

The Ideas and Beliefs of Ancient Greece

Sally Cowan

Contents

CHAPTER 1

The Rise of Ancient Greece

Around 2800 years ago, farming and trade began to develop in ancient Greece.

Traders became wealthy and life was good for many people. The population increased, and a few towns grew into big cities. Towns were set up along the coast, and from there the Greeks settled in many places around the Mediterranean Sea.

From around 500 **BC** to 300 BC, ancient Greek culture and **influence** was at its peak.

The ancient Greeks were very interested in the arts, and they produced many beautiful artworks.
They also created an alphabet, from which later European alphabets developed.
Many artworks and writings from ancient Greece still exist today.

The Greeks also developed ideas and beliefs to help them explain many things about life.

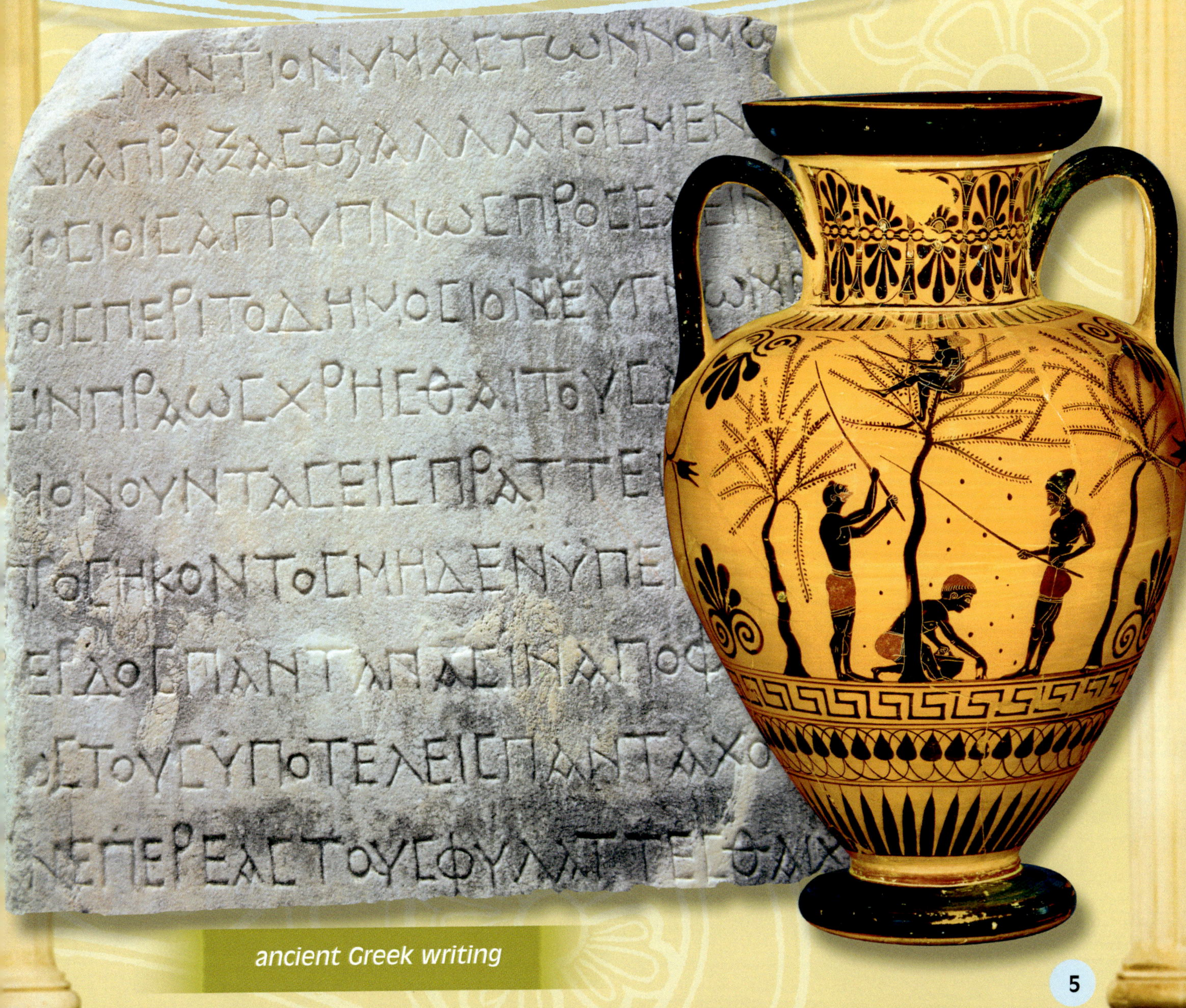

ancient Greek writing

CHAPTER 2

Ideas About Government

By around 500 BC, the large cities ruled over the smaller towns around them.

They had become **city-states**.

The ancient Greeks did not think of themselves as "Greeks", but as citizens of their city-state.

Two of the most famous city-states were Athens and Sparta.

Athens – The First Democracy

Most ancient societies were ruled by a powerful king, but the city-state of Athens was different.

It was a **democracy**.

The ancient Athenians believed that the citizens should have a say in how their government worked.

Citizens could vote about laws and elect people to government.

They could even vote to have people who were not doing a good job removed from government.

A New Idea

Athens is believed to be the first democracy in the world.
Only Athenian citizens could vote and take part in government.
However, only men could become Athenian citizens.

Sparta – A Military State

Unlike Athens, Sparta was a **military** city-state ruled by two kings and a small group of men.

One king stayed in Sparta to look after the government, while the other king went off to war.

Spartans at war

The Spartans valued strength above everything else, because they spent a lot of time fighting wars to protect their lands.

All boys were sent to train as soldiers at the age of seven. At 20, the young men became full-time soldiers of the state.

Girls took part in sports to become strong. The Spartans believed that strong women would have strong, healthy babies.

A Strong Belief

Spartans believed that babies should be strong from birth. A group of Spartan elders decided if a newborn baby was strong enough to live. Babies that were considered weak were left on a mountain to die.

a statue of a Spartan king

CHAPTER 3

Ideas About Learning

Philosophy

The ancient Greeks invented a new area of learning called philosophy.

Philosophers used reason to understand the world and put forward ideas about how people should live their lives.

The Athenians believed that it was important to develop the mind through learning.

The philosopher Plato started a famous school of philosophy in Athens, called the Platonic Academy.

A New Idea

The word "philosophy" comes from the Greek words *phileîn* ("to love") and *sophía* ("wisdom"). So "philosophy" means "love of wisdom".

philosophers discussing ideas

Mathematics and Science

The Greeks thought of new ideas in the areas of mathematics and science.

Some of the rules of mathematics that they discovered are still used today.

Pythagoras's rule is used to make mathematical calculations about triangles.

Aristotle

An ancient Greek philosopher called Aristotle started botany, the scientific study of plants.

Medicine

There were new ideas about medicine, too.

A Greek doctor called Hippocrates is known as the first doctor to challenge the ancient belief that sickness was a punishment from the gods.

He realised that diet and lifestyle were important in keeping the body healthy.

Hippocrates

THE OATH

I SWEAR by Apollo the physician and Esculapius & Health & All-heal & all the gods & goddesses that according to my ability & judgement I WILL KEEP THIS OATH & this stipulation—to reckon him who taught me this Art equally dear to me as my parents to share my substance with him & relieve his necessities if required, to look upon his offspring in the same footing as my own brothers & to teach them this Art, if they shall wish to learn it, WITHOUT FEE OR STIPULATION & that by precept lecture & every other mode of instruction, I will impart a knowledge of the Art to my own sons & those of my teachers & to disciples bound by a stipulation & oath ACCORDING TO THE LAW OF MEDICINE but to none others. I will follow the system of regimen which according to my ability & judgement, I consider FOR THE BENEFIT OF MY PATIENTS & abstain from whatever is deleterious & mischievous. I will give no deadly medicine to any one if asked nor suggest any such counsel & in like manner I will not give to a woman a pessary to produce abortion. WITH PURITY & WITH HOLINESS I WILL PASS MY LIFE & PRACTICE MY ART. I will not cut persons laboring under the stone, but will leave this to be done by men who are practitioners of this work. Into whatever houses I enter, I will go into them for the benefit of the sick & will abstain from every voluntary act of mischief & corruption AND FURTHER from the seduction of females or males, of freemen & slaves. Whatever in connection with my professional practice or not in connection with it, I see or hear, in the life of men which ought not to be spoken of abroad, I WILL NOT DIVULGE as reckoning that all such should be kept secret. While I continue to keep this Oath unviolated, may it be granted to me to enjoy life & the practice of the Art respected by all men in all times! But should I trespass & violate this Oath, may the reverse be my lot!

ΙΠΠΟΚΡΑΤΗΣ

the Hippocratic Oath

A Healing Belief

The Hippocratic Oath is a promise to save lives and treat people in a responsible way. Today, when doctors begin practising medicine, they sometimes still take the Hippocratic Oath.

Hippocrates examined many sick people.
He was first to describe some diseases and to keep records for other doctors to use.

Doctors began to treat people with medicines made from plants.
But many people still believed that only the gods had the power to heal them.

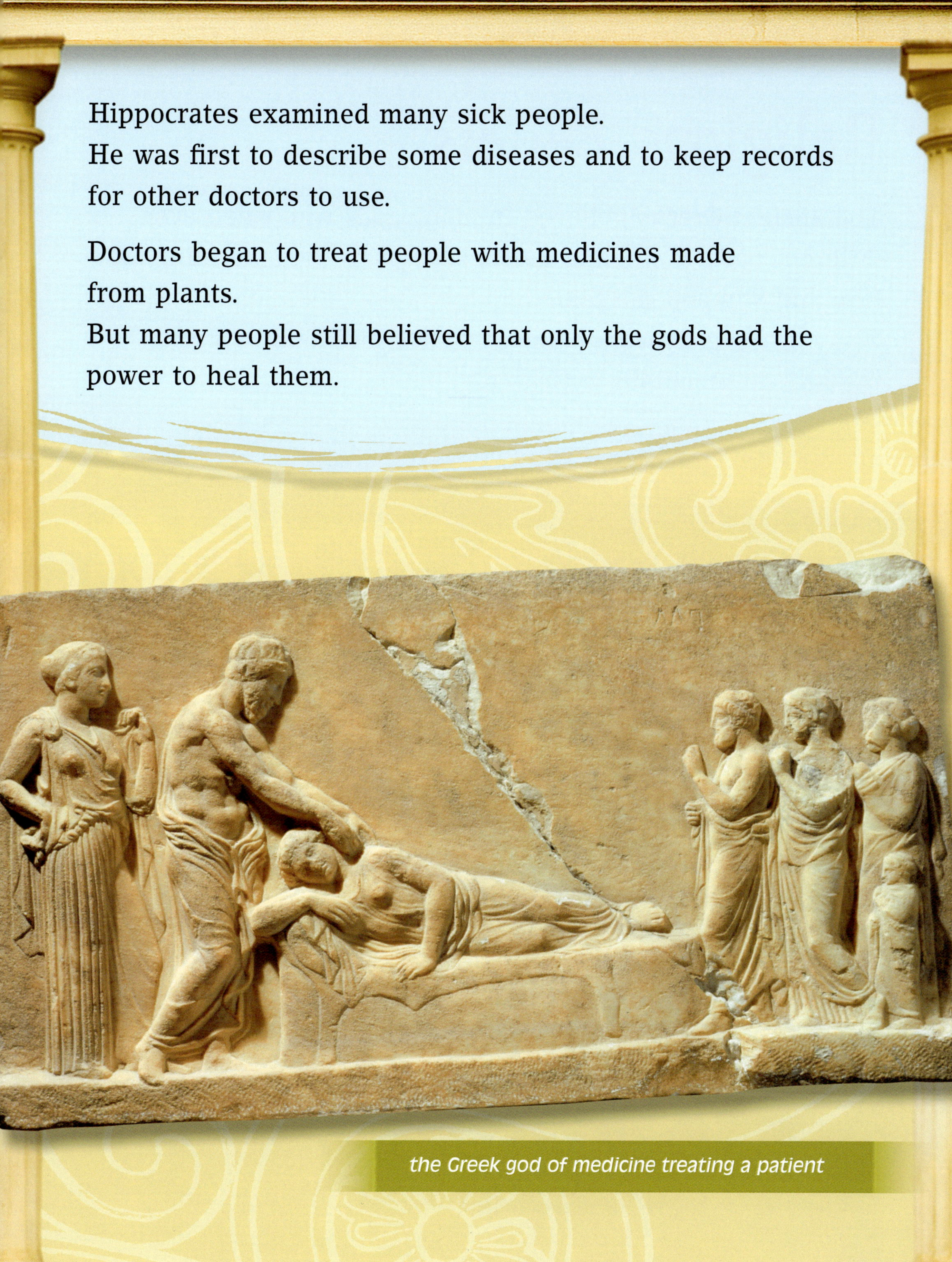

the Greek god of medicine treating a patient

CHAPTER 4

Religious Beliefs

The ancient Greeks believed in many gods who ruled over different parts of life and Earth, such as hunting, farming, war, love, the Sun and the sea.

Many of the gods were believed to live on Mount Olympus, the highest mountain in Greece.

Zeus, the king of the ancient Greek gods

The Parthenon was built for Athena, the goddess of wisdom, war, arts and crafts.

People thought the gods could not die because their blood was different from ordinary people's blood.
But people also believed that the gods could marry, have children and affect people's lives.
For this reason, people wanted to have the gods on their side.

The Greeks built great stone **temples** in which to **worship** the different gods.

People held festivals and left offerings of food and drink at the temples to please the gods.

Sometimes, they **sacrificed** animals at the temples.

Some of the meat was burned so that the smoke could drift up to reach the gods.

The rest of the meat was cooked and eaten by the people in a great feast.

In this artwork, an ox is about to be sacrificed to please Artemis, the goddess of hunting.

Everyday Offerings

The ancient Greeks also made offerings of food and drink to the gods at ordinary mealtimes. People did this by burning food in the fireplace and pouring drink on the floor.

Sometimes festivals included plays about the adventures of the gods.
The ancient Greeks loved theatre, dancing and music, not only as entertainment, but also as important ways to please the gods.

a play being performed at the theatre of the god Dionysus

CHAPTER 5

The Olympic Games

Many ancient Greeks believed that a healthy lifestyle was very important, so sport and keeping fit were a big part of ancient Greek culture.

In 776 BC, the first Olympic Games were held at Olympia. Only Greek men could take part, and every four years they came from all over Greece to watch and compete.

The warrior race was an ancient Olympic event. The athletes had to wear full battle gear weighing around 25 kilograms.

If any of the Greek city-states were at war during the Olympics, they stopped fighting until the games were finished. This was so that everyone could safely come together to enjoy the games.

an ancient Greek stadium

A Healthy Idea

The ancient Greeks invented the gymnasium, a place where people could go to keep fit.

It was a great honour for athletes to compete at the games. They took part in running races and other sports. There were many rules about fair play, and cheats were fined or even beaten up.

Competition was strong between the city-states. The Greeks believed that winning at the Olympics was one of the greatest honours for an athlete and his city-state.

This vase shows ancient Greek athletes competing.

A crowd cheers a winning athlete.

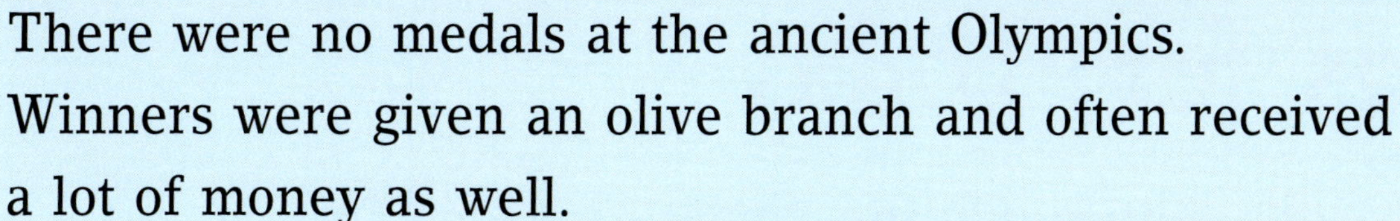

There were no medals at the ancient Olympics. Winners were given an olive branch and often received a lot of money as well.

An Old Idea Revived

In the late 1800s, Olympia was dug up by archaeologists. People became interested in the spirit of competition of the ancient Greeks, and the modern Olympic Games began in 1896.

an olive branch

An athlete competes at the modern Olympic Games.

CHAPTER 6

Ideas for Today

In the second century BC, the Romans invaded Greece and took control of it.

The Romans became the most powerful people in Europe, but they were impressed with Greek culture and helped to spread it.

Today the influence of ancient Greece is still found around the world in

- large public buildings
- democratic government

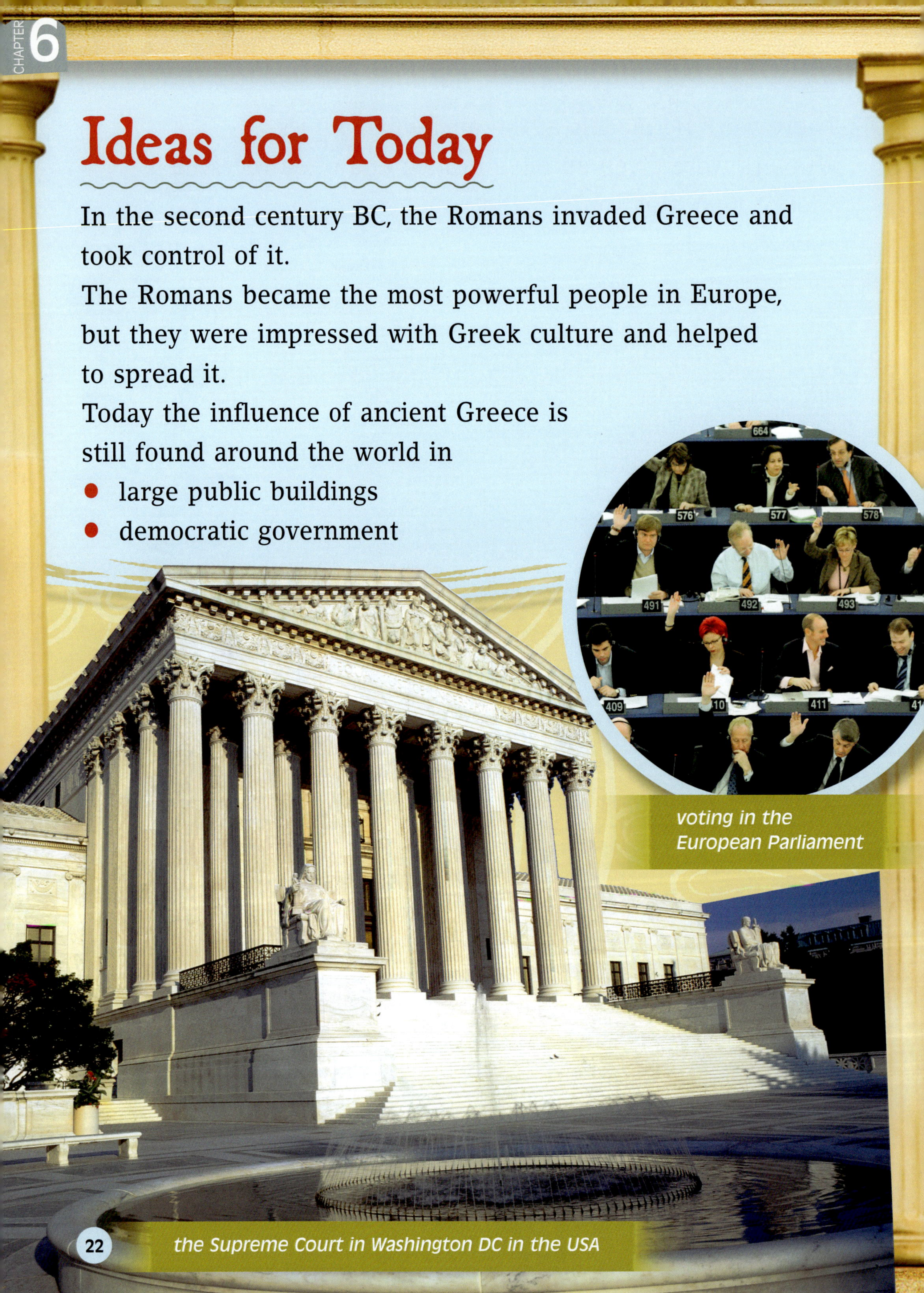

voting in the European Parliament

the Supreme Court in Washington DC in the USA

- ideas and beliefs about science and philosophy
- ideas about fitness and sport
- the arts.

Ancient Greek maths is still used today.

a modern gym

Many ancient Greek plays are still performed today.

Glossary

BC stands for "before Christ", and refers to any year before the birth of Jesus Christ

city-states large areas of land surrounding and controlled by powerful cities

democracy a kind of government where the leaders are elected by the citizens

influence a long-lasting or important effect

military of or relating to the army

sacrificed killed as an offering to the gods

temples buildings where gods were worshipped

worship to show respect to a god

Index